THE QUEEN

Based on the motion picture *The Queen*
written by Peter Morgan

www.thequeenmovie.co.uk

LEVEL 3

SCHOLASTIC

Adapted by: Rod Smith

Fact Files written by: Rod Smith

Publisher: Jacquie Bloese

Commissioning Editor: Helen Parker

Editor: Cheryl Pelteret

Designer: Dawn Wilson

Picture research: Emma Bree

Photo credits:
Page 5: Photodisc; Travel Library/Rex; S. Barbour/Getty Images.
Page 13: S. O. Groki/AFP/Getty Images.
Pages 17 & 39: P. Vicente/AFP/Getty Images.
Page 51: B. Batchelor/PA.
Page 57: R. Beck/AFP/Getty Images.
Pages 58 & 59: M. Heyhow, I. Waldie, A. Wyld, C. DeSouza/ AFP/Getty Images.
Pages 60 & 61: P. Vicente/AFP, EPA, P. Macdiarmid/Getty Images; Rex.

Published by Scholastic Ltd. 2009

Mary Glasgow Magazines (Scholastic Ltd)
Euston House
24 Eversholt Street
London NW1 IDB

Printed in Singapore. Reprinted in 2010.

Contents

The ROYALS

QUEEN ELIZABETH II ►
is the Queen of England. She lives in Buckingham Palace, in London, and spends holidays with her family in Balmoral, Scotland.

PRINCE PHILIP is the Queen's husband. He enjoys country sports. He doesn't agree with Tony Blair about making Britain more modern.

PRINCE CHARLES is the eldest son of the Queen and Prince Philip. He was married to Diana Spencer.

THE QUEEN MOTHER often advises her daughter on the best thing to do. The Queen is very close to her mother.

ROBIN JANVRIN is the Queen's Private Secretary. He works in her office and deals with the media.

The POLITICIANS

TONY BLAIR
is Britain's new Prime Minister. He is young, popular with the people, and he wants to make the country more modern.

CHERIE BLAIR
is Tony Blair's wife. She doesn't think Britain needs a royal family.

ALISTAIR CAMPBELL is Tony Blair's Press Secretary. It is his job to present a good opinion of Tony Blair and the Labour Party in the newspapers and on TV.

Tony and Cherie Blair

PLACES

BUCKINGHAM PALACE
Buckingham Palace is the Queen and Royal Family's home in London.

BALMORAL
Balmoral is the Queen's home in Scotland. The Queen and the Royal Family spend their holidays there.

DOWNING STREET
Number 10 Downing Street, is the London home and office of the British Prime Minister.

THE QUEEN

INTRODUCTION

The story of *The Queen* begins in May, 1997, with the election of a new British government. The leader of this new government, is Prime Minister, Tony Blair.

The Prime Minister's government is a group of people, called a 'party', who agree with his or her opinions. For the past eighteen years, the Conservative Party has ruled the country. Now people have voted for change, and Tony Blair's Labour Party has won the election.

Although the Queen cannot vote, Britain's government is formed in her name. The Prime Minister regularly visits the Queen in Buckingham Palace, her home in London. They discuss ideas and opinions on state business.

Tony Blair wants to make Britain more modern. This idea isn't popular with people who belong to 'the Establishment'. These are people in very high positions; they include leaders in the church and other national institutions with a long history in the country. They believe in tradition and are slow to accept modern ideas. Queen Elizabeth II is an important part of the Establishment. She is a living example of the importance of tradition in British life. Part of this tradition is to always act with dignity and to keep feelings private.

Since she became Queen in 1953, Elizabeth's rule was generally calm. Things began to change in the mid-1980s. She then had to face two problems. The first was the growing attention of the media on famous people like the Royal Family. The second began with the marriage of her son, Prince Charles, to Diana Spencer, in 1981.

During the following ten years, Princess Diana, as the world knew her, became one of the most famous and popular women in the world.

Charles and Diana had two sons: William, born in 1982, and Harry, born two years later. By this time there were problems in the marriage. Charles had always been in love with someone else – a married woman called Camilla Parker-Bowles. This made Diana very unhappy. The media became interested in the private lives of Charles and Diana, and, after some time, Diana spoke publicly about her problems. The Queen and the rest of the Establishment disliked this. But people felt sorry for Diana and she became even more popular with them. Charles and Diana finally divorced in 1996.

But their divorce did not end the Queen's problems. A year later, there would be even worse problems for her…

CHAPTER 1
A new government

It was the May 1, 1997. Britain's election was over and its people had chosen a new Prime Minister. His name was Tony Blair – the youngest Prime Minister of the century. Mr Blair promised to make the country more modern and the people agreed with his views. Now he and his wife, Cherie, were on their way to Buckingham Palace to see the Queen. She would ask Mr Blair to form a government.

As their car drove through the main gates, Tony Blair turned to his wife and said, 'It's strange, but I'm feeling quite nervous.'

'I don't know why,' said Cherie. 'You've met her quite a few times already.'

'Yes, but I've never been alone with her before.'

'You'll be all right. Don't forget that the whole country has just voted for you as their Prime Minister. They didn't vote for the Queen.'

'Yes, but she's still … you know, … the *Queen*.'

The Queen's Private Secretary, Robin Janvrin, was looking out of the window of the Queen's meeting room on the first floor of Buckingham Palace.

'The Prime Minister and his wife are arriving now, Ma'am*,' he said.

'Mr Blair is not the Prime Minister yet, Robin. Remember, I have to ask him first.'

'Of course, Ma'am.'

The Queen had met Blair before but she didn't really know him. She wondered about his personality. 'I don't know what to think of him,' she said. 'What's your opinion, Robin?'

'He's difficult to understand, Ma'am,' Janvrin replied. 'His family and his education is quite traditional. However, his wife is certainly not a fan of the Royal Family. And Mr Blair has promised to make Britain more modern.'

'Oh dear. Is he going to try and make us more modern, too?'

'It's possible, Ma'am. I was told that in Downing Street now, they address people by their first names.'

'You mean people call him "Tony"?'

'Yes, Ma'am.'

'Oh dear! I hope he doesn't try to do that here. Did we send him a protocol list?'

* 'Ma'am' and 'Your Majesty' are polite ways to address the Queen.

At the main door of the palace, one of the Queen's servants met Mr and Mrs Blair and led them upstairs. On the way, he was telling them the rules of how to act when they were with the Queen. 'When I knock at the door, we enter. We don't wait for her to call us in. And remember, you must never show your back to Her Majesty.'

'Right,' said Blair. He looked at Cherie, who tried not to laugh.

The servant offered Cherie Blair a seat in the hall. She sat down and waited. The man knocked at the door, then opened it and stepped to one side as Blair entered the room.

'It's lovely to meet you again, Mr Blair,' the Queen said, in welcome. 'And well done. Your children must be very proud of you. You've got three children, haven't you?'

'Yes, Your Majesty.'

'That's wonderful. Please, do sit down.'

'Thank you, Ma'am.'

'My job as Queen is to advise and guide you. Also, I will let your government know if I see any problems ahead. I will do this during our weekly meetings.'

'Your opinion will always be very valuable to me, Ma'am.'

'Thank you, Mr Blair. And now, I think we have some business to complete.'

Tony Blair didn't know what she meant. Then he suddenly realised and went down on his knees. He spoke nervously.

'Yes, Ma'am. Er .... Your Majesty,' he began. 'The people of Britain have chosen me as their new Prime Minister. So I would like to ask for your agreement to form a ...'

The Queen shook her head and smiled. 'No, no, Mr Blair. It is me who asks you the question.'

'Oh … er, yes, of course …. Your Majesty.'

'As your Queen, I invite you to become Prime Minister and to form a government in my name.'

Blair looked at the Queen. 'Now what do I do?' he thought. He was feeling more and more nervous. After waiting for a few seconds, the Queen continued softly, 'If you agree, Mr Blair, it is normal to say *yes*.'

'Oh, then 'yes', Your Majesty.'

Their business was over. The Queen called her servant. Seconds later, he brought Cherie Blair into the room.

'Mrs Blair,' said the Queen, shaking Cherie's hand. 'It's very nice to see you again. You must be very proud. And very tired, too, I think. You probably feel like a holiday. Are you going anywhere this summer?'

'France,' said Cherie Blair. She didn't address the Queen correctly.

The Queen noticed. Blair noticed, too, and said quickly,

'Are you going to Balmoral, Ma'am?'

The Queen smiled. 'Yes. It's in a wonderful part of Scotland. There, you can forget the world and all its problems.'

At that moment, Janvrin came into the room. He went up to the Queen and whispered something in her ear. The Queen looked serious. When Janvrin had left the room, she turned to Mr and Mrs Blair and said, 'I'm sorry, but I'm afraid I'll have to end our meeting now.'

'What do you think Janvrin told the Queen?' Blair asked Cherie as they walked back downstairs. 'She looked rather upset.'

Cherie gave a short laugh. 'Something to do with Princess Diana, I expect.'

CHAPTER 2
A terrible accident

It was late summer. Princess Diana had often been in the news. The main stories were about her and her friend, Mr. Dodi Fayed. It seemed that the couple were in love. Newspaper pictures showed them together on one of Dodi Fayed's boats in the Mediterranean. But there were also stories about all the charity work Diana did to help people all over the world. These included sick children, prisoners' families and people with war injuries.

Princess Diana doing charity work

The Queen and the Royal Family thought that Princess Diana's charity work was a good thing. But they didn't like the media attention that Diana received. For them, charity was about doing good things quietly. With Diana, this was impossible.

In private life, the Queen thought that 'living quietly' was even more important. But since her divorce, Diana continued to talk to the media about her problems with Charles and the Royal Family. This and her charity work made her someone people could understand. She was the same as them – she had problems and difficulties, too. And she was a good person. Many people wanted to be like Princess Diana. She became their perfect woman. Photographers and reporters followed her everywhere. They would do almost anything to get a story about her or a photo of her. Until one day, at the end of August, when something terrible happened.

In the early hours of the morning of August 31, Diana and Dodi left their hotel in Paris with their driver and a guard. Newspaper reporters and photographers were waiting outside on motorbikes.

Diana and Dodi were tired of being followed everywhere. They tried to escape the media by going out the back entrance of the hotel. But they were seen, and the waiting photographers raced after them, their motorbikes speeding through the night streets. Diana's driver drove faster and faster. In the end, he was unable to manage the car. It crashed. Dodi Fayed was killed and Diana was taken to hospital. She had very serious injuries.

In Britain, Robin Janvrin was the first person to receive news of the crash from the British Ambassador in Paris. Janvrin was staying with the Royal Family at Balmoral. After his short telephone conversation with the Ambassador he went to give the Queen the bad news.

'I'm sorry, Your Majesty,' Janvrin said. 'But our Ambassador in Paris has just telephoned. It's about Princess Diana. She's been in a car accident in Paris.'

In London, Tony Blair was also woken by the news. He

put the phone down and turned to Cherie. 'It's Diana,' he said. 'She's been in a car crash in Paris.'

'How bad is it?' asked Cherie.

'Very bad. It seems Dodi Fayed is dead.'

The whole Royal Family was now awake. They sat watching the latest news on TV.

'Princess Diana is now in hospital in the south east of Paris,' the news reader was saying. 'She has several injuries, including a broken arm ... '

Charles wanted to go to Paris immediately. The Queen Mother told him to travel in the royal plane. The Queen didn't like that idea. Because Charles and Diana were divorced, Diana was no longer in the Royal Family so she didn't think Charles should use the royal plane.

Charles was angry. 'She's no longer in the Royal Family, but she's still your grandchildren's mother!' he said.

At that moment, Robin Janvrin came into the room. He looked very serious. 'I'm afraid I have some very bad news from our Ambassador in Paris, Ma'am. Princess Diana has died in hospital.'

Charles put his hands over his face. The Queen turned very pale.

Tony Blair had also been told of Diana's death. He ordered his Press Secretary, Alistair Campbell, to change the Prime Minister's plans for the week. Diana's death was far more important than anything else.

'I'll have to give a public speech,' Blair said.

Campbell looked down at his notebook. 'Of course. I've already written a few things down.' He read out what he wanted to say. "Diana was "the People's Princess".'

In Balmoral, Charles was giving his two young sons, William and Harry, the news of their mother's death. He kissed them and told them that Princess Diana would want them to be brave.

When Charles left their bedroom, the Queen was waiting outside. She went to put her arm around her son's shoulder but pulled it back before they touched. Charles didn't seem to notice. 'Is it still a problem if I bring their mother's body back in one of our royal planes?' he asked her in a flat voice.

'Of course not,' the Queen replied. She was upset that Charles was still angry with her about that matter.

After he left, she spoke to one of the servants. 'I don't want the children to listen to the radio, read the newspapers, or watch television. Please make sure all those things are taken away.'

'Yes, Ma'am,' the servant replied.

CHAPTER 3
A private sadness

News of Diana's death was now public. For Britain and the world, it was hard to believe. Outside Buckingham Palace and Kensington Palace, Diana's home, people were laying flowers. Most people were crying and looking very upset.

Flowers outside Kensington Palace

People wondered about Charles and Diana's children – Prince William and Prince Harry. How were they feeling? What help were they getting? A large number of people expected the Queen to make a public speech. But, so far, there was only silence from the Royal Family.

This was not the case with Tony Blair. In a few hours' time, he would speak on TV. From his home, he checked his notes on the phone with Campbell.

The first person to speak in public was Diana's brother, Earl Spencer. He spoke from outside his home in South Africa. In Spencer's opinion, the Press had killed his sister. They had wanted photographs. They had been ready to do almost anything to get them – including chasing Diana's car. These selfish acts were the reason that his sister was now dead. 'The Press,' said Spencer, 'have blood on their hands.'

In Britain, Tony Blair didn't think he should be the first important person to talk in public about Diana's death. He thought the Royal Family should do that. He decided to speak to the Queen.

The Royal Family were having breakfast in Balmoral when Blair called.

The Queen took the phone call in her study.

After saying how sorry he was about Diana's death, Blair asked if the Queen was going to speak to the people of Britain.

'Certainly not,' she replied. 'This is a private matter. I hope you understand that.'

Blair felt uncomfortable. 'Er ... yes. Er ... it's probably a bit early, but have you thought about the funeral?'

'Yes, we have,' said the Queen sharply. 'Diana's family would like it to be private. They made that very clear.'

Blair looked up from the phone at Cherie, then continued, 'Er, Diana, as you know, Your Majesty, was very popular with people all over the world. Don't you think a public funeral might give them the chance to … '

'To what, Mr Blair?'

'Well … to show their sadness.'

The Queen sat very straight. 'Sadness?' she said. 'This will be a family funeral, Mr Blair, not a public show. If Diana's life had been more private, there might not be a funeral at all. And now, if there is nothing else, I must go. The children need me.'

'Yes, of course. Er … goodbye, Your Majesty.' Blair put the phone down and turned to Cherie. 'She's not going to give a public speech, and she wants a private funeral.'

Cherie wasn't surprised. 'What did you expect?' she said. 'The Queen hated Diana.'

'Well, I think she's making a big mistake,' said Blair.

The Queen was upset by her conversation with Blair. In her opinion, it was important to face sadness in private, with dignity. She had always thought this was part of her duty as Queen. But in Blair's 'modern' Britain, it seemed that public shows of feeling were necessary. This was something she didn't understand. But this wasn't the time to try and understand these things. Her grandchildren were more important right now.

Her thoughts turned to William and Harry. One thing she felt sure about: too much attention on their mother's death would upset them more than necessary. They needed to keep busy and do things.

This was something Prince Philip understood. 'I could take them for a walk up to Craggy Head,' he suggested. Craggy Head was a beautiful place in the country, not far from Balmoral. Some of Scotland's most interesting wild animals could often be seen there.

'That's a good idea,' said the Queen. 'But no guns, Philip. We don't want any excited newspaper photographers taking pictures.'

In Paris, Charles had gone to the hospital where Diana had died. He stood in the room where her body lay in an open coffin. He looked down at her and felt very sad. Diana had not been perfect, but she had been a wonderful, loving mother. The children would miss her terribly.

Back in Britain, Blair was giving a public speech about Diana in front of the TV cameras.

'Princess Diana touched the lives of people all over the world,' he said. 'Where there was sadness, she brought hope. People everywhere liked her and loved her. They thought of her as "the People's Princess". And that is how we will always remember her.'

The people of Britain liked Blair's speech. It made them wonder about the Queen. When was she going to speak to them?

All over the world, other important people were also speaking about Princess Diana.

'I will always be glad that I knew the Princess,' US President, Bill Clinton, said sadly.

In South Africa, the country's President, Nelson Mandela, also talked of the good work Princess Diana had done for charity and how much he and the world would miss her.

But, more than anything else, Diana belonged to ordinary people. The television showed pictures of them in cities all over the world laying flowers for the Princess. Blair was right. Diana *was* 'the People's Princess'.

CHAPTER 4
The meeting

One thing soon became clear. It would not be possible for Diana to have a private funeral. She was too popular. Up to now, public funerals were only for people in the Royal Family.

The Queen would not want this tradition broken. However, in this case, public opinion was more important.

The man who had to arrange the funeral was called Lord Airlie. He tried to explain these difficulties to Tony Blair on the phone.

Blair couldn't understand Lord Airlie's worries about breaking tradition. Blair saw himself as a modern leader. To him, Lord Airlie sounded like a man locked in the past.

They agreed on a meeting between important people in the government and the Establishment. It would be in Buckingham Palace at ten o'clock the following morning.

Tony Blair left for the airport. He had to be there to welcome Prince Charles back from Paris.

Charles stepped off the plane and shook Blair's hand. But his thoughts were far away. 'It was amazing,' he said. 'People stood up as we drove past. They took off their hats. This was Paris, one of the busiest cities in the world and the streets were silent.'

'I'm sure it will be no different here, Sir,' said Blair.

'Yes, I think you're right.' Charles seemed to notice Blair for the first time. 'Look,' he said. 'My mother would prefer a private funeral. What's your opinion on that?'

Blair smiled politely. 'I think that might be difficult, Sir.'

'I agree.' Charles seemed unsure of what to say, then

continued. 'You must understand that my mother grew up during the war. Things were very different then. It was important to be strong and not show your feelings. But what Britain needs at this time is a leader with a more modern view, if you understand?'

'Yes, I think I do,' replied Blair. 'I'm pleased that we both share the same opinion.'

As they again shook hands, Blair wondered if Charles was being honest. Or was there another reason he was acting in such a friendly way? Perhaps it didn't matter, he thought.

The two men watched in quiet dignity as Diana's coffin was taken from the plane.

In Balmoral, Diana's death was still the main subject for discussion. Prince Philip wanted to change the subject. He turned to the Queen Mother. 'Someone said they'd seen a huge stag up at Craggy Head, today.'

The Queen Mother looked surprised. 'Really? We haven't had a really big one up here for years.'

The Queen realised that Philip and her mother were trying to change the subject from the unhappy news to something else. But in the middle of all the TV reports of Diana's death, their conversation seemed strange. She watched the news pictures of Blair welcoming Charles at the airport. Charles was acting in a very friendly way. At one point he whispered something in Blair's ear. The Queen wondered what he was saying. She looked worried.

Prince Philip hadn't noticed. 'I thought the boys and I could look for that stag, tomorrow,' he said. 'It's important to keep them busy.'

The Queen was suddenly interested. 'Really? I hope you're not taking them to shoot it. It's still a bit soon for that sort of thing.'

'Oh, I don't know,' Philip replied. 'I think any activity that gets them out the house is a good idea.'

'Well, don't take any guns, that's all.'

The Queen turned back to the TV. It was showing Blair's speech about Diana. She looked at the screen in disbelief. Finally she stood up. 'I can't listen to any more of this,' she said. 'I'm going to bed.'

The next day, Blair wanted to practise a speech to the country about his government's future plans. So he sent Alistair Campbell to the meeting with Lord Airlie. Alone in his office, Blair read his speech out loud:

'I want to make this country more modern. I want to put new life into old ways of doing things. Up until now, special groups of people have been in a better position to enjoy life than others. I want to change that. I want to make that possible for everyone.'

Three hours later, Blair's office door opened and Alistair Campbell came into the room. He looked upset and threw a pile of newspapers on Blair's desk.

'How was the meeting?' Blair asked.

'Don't ask,' Campbell replied. He looked angry. 'I thought the Queen was crazy. But they are worse. I've never been so bored. They kept talking about protocol. Every little thing has to be done in the right way. It took them hours to make a decision.' His face suddenly brightened as he looked at the newspapers on Blair's desk. 'But it's not all bad news. The Press say that you're the only person who understands the country's feelings. That's thanks to the nice little title I gave you for Diana: "the People's Princess". Don't forget where it came from, will you?'

'OK, Alistair. But what about the funeral? Is it going to be public?'

'Yeah,' said Campbell. 'And it's going to be huge.'

'Have they told the Queen?'

'They'll probably send some nervous little servant up there to give her the news.'

Blair smiled but, inside, he, too, was feeling nervous.

The Queen was not pleased when she received news that Diana would be given a public funeral. She was even less pleased when Janvrin gave her the plans for how it would be arranged. They were the same as the plans for the Queen Mother's funeral.

Janvrin tried to explain. 'This is the only funeral plan that we have already practised, Ma'am. Lord Airlie said there isn't time to arrange anything different. But, of course, it wouldn't be exactly the same as your funeral, Ma'am,' he went on quickly, looking at the Queen Mother. 'For one thing, the main guests wouldn't be world leaders. They would be film and TV actors and other, er ... celebrities.'

The Queen Mother turned pale. 'Celebrities?' she asked.

Janvrin looked down at the floor without replying.

'Did you have anything else to tell us?' asked the Queen.

'Er, no, Ma'am, just that the police thought a book for people to sign would be a good idea. They could also write a few words to say how sorry they were about the Princess's death. It's partly a way of making it easier for the police to manage the crowds. Oh, and the flowers outside Buckingham Palace, Ma'am. They don't want to move them for the Changing of the Guard*. They suggest sending the Guards through the North Gate.'

'Yes, of course,' said the Queen. Things were happening so quickly, she felt she had no choice.

Janvrin stepped back, turned and quietly left the room.

* The 'Changing of the Guard' is when there is a change of the groups of guards who protect Buckingham Palace.

CHAPTER 5
Charles disagrees

The public was waiting for a sign that the Royal Family cared about Diana. Many people thought that the flag should be flying at half-mast* over Buckingham Palace to show this. But there was no flag at all, and the Queen had not returned to London to speak about Diana's death. Did this mean that the Royal Family had no feelings about Diana? Some people thought so, and criticisms began to appear in the media.

'Where's the Queen?' an angry man was saying on TV. 'She should be in London, talking to the people. There isn't even a flag flying to show that Diana was important!'

Watching the TV report, Tony Blair realised he would have to speak to the Queen about the flag. He would also try again to get her to make a public speech about Diana. Or perhaps Charles could speak to her about it ... ? He

* A flag is flown at half-mast (half its full height) to show someone important has died.

remembered again, a conversation he'd had earlier that morning with the Prince's Private Secretary.

'The Prince thinks that you are both modern men. You have the same opinion on many things. He is sure you could work well together during this difficult time.'

Again, Blair wondered about Charles. After his conversation with the Prince's Private Secretary, he'd discussed the matter with people in his office. Why was Charles being so helpful? And why was he going against his mother's wishes? 'Because he doesn't want the people to hate him,' someone had suggested. 'He is next in line to be King.' Campbell said it was because the Prince was afraid that someone – perhaps one of Diana's fans – would shoot him. Blair thought that this was probably true: Charles had already asked for extra policemen to protect him during the funeral.

Back in Scotland, Charles, his mother and her two dogs were driving along a forest road near Balmoral.

'You know, I wish I'd taken the boys with me to Paris,' Charles said suddenly. 'That's what Diana would do if she were alive and I had died.'

The Queen turned to Charles and said sharply, 'And let the boys face the media? That would be a terrible thing to do. It's much better for them to stay here.'

'Look, I know you were unhappy about some of the things Diana did, but she was a wonderful mother. She loved those boys and was never afraid to show her feelings.'

'That was certainly true whenever a photographer was near,' replied the Queen.

'Perhaps,' Charles said, 'but – amazingly – her

weaknesses only made the public love her more. Yet our weaknesses make them hate us. Why is that?'

He suddenly remembered something and added, 'Yesterday, for example, I heard a bang as we drove Diana's coffin through London. I thought someone was trying to shoot me.'

The Queen was tired of the conversation. She stopped the car. 'You go on without me, Charles. I feel like a walk. I'll take the dogs back to Balmoral.'

Charles knew his mother was upset but he didn't want to disagree with her. As the Queen walked off with the dogs he climbed into the driving seat and drove away.

That evening, while she was still thinking about her conversation with Charles, the Queen sat in her room, watching TV. It was showing an old film of Diana talking to a reporter.

'I want to be queen of people's hearts,' Diana was saying. 'But I'll never be accepted as Queen of England. The Establishment doesn't want someone like me.'

Prince Philip came into the room. The Queen told him about her earlier conversation with Charles.

'He's changed his opinion rather suddenly,' Philip replied. 'He never said Diana was such a wonderful mother before.'

'No, but maybe he's right about some things.'

'What things?' asked Philip.

'That the problems between us and Diana were partly our fault. We both wanted him to marry Diana, remember.'

'Well, she was a nice girl then,' Philip replied.

On the TV screen there was a picture of Camilla Parker-Bowles. Diana was talking about the problems this woman had brought to Diana and Charles's marriage.

'There were three of us in that marriage,' she said. 'It was a bit crowded.'

Philip pointed at the picture of Camilla on the TV screen. 'And I thought Charles would stop seeing *her*. Or at least, that Diana would keep quiet about it. Isn't that what everyone does?'

The Queen didn't reply. She felt a little hurt by what Philip had just said.

Philip didn't realise he had upset her. He just wanted to get away from the TV. 'I can't listen to this anymore,' he said. 'I'm going to bed.'

'Did you get your stag?' the Queen asked.

'Not yet. Tomorrow, I hope – with a bit of luck.' He kissed the Queen goodnight and left the room.

CHAPTER 6
An unpopular queen

Tony Blair was worried. There was no sign of the Queen coming to London. And the criticisms were getting worse. He sat watching TV with his wife. People were speaking to reporters outside Buckingham Palace.

'The Royal Family never liked Diana,' one woman was saying. 'It's because she didn't always do what the Establishment wanted her to do.'

Cherie turned to her husband. 'You see? People are finally realising what the Royal Family are really like.'

'What do you mean?'

'They don't belong in the modern world. They're also expensive. The Queen costs the country 40 million pounds a year. It's time for a change.'

'You mean we should stop having a royal family?'

'Why not?'

'The people of Britain wouldn't like it. The idea's just … crazy.'

'I read that one in six people no longer want a royal family,' Cherie continued.

'That's just the newspapers making trouble,' Blair said.

'No, it's not. People want change. And they want you to give it to them.'

Blair didn't reply. He was thinking very seriously about what Cherie had said.

The following day, there were more criticisms of the Queen in the newspapers. Janvrin sat in his office reading the headlines. They were nearly all bad: 'The Royal Family is not like us.'; 'Whose advice are they taking?'; 'It's time for change!' Janvrin looked worried.

Blair was also worried by the criticisms of the Queen. He was reading a speech Campbell had written for him when his secretary came into the room. 'Who wrote all that?' he asked, pointing to the newspapers. 'Where does it come from?'

'The people,' his secretary replied. 'They want change.'

'Right,' said Blair. 'This has gone far enough.' He told her to leave the room. After she'd left, he closed the door and picked up the phone.

The Queen was drinking tea when Blair rang.

'Good morning, Your Majesty. I'm sorry to trouble you, but have you seen today's newspapers?' Blair asked.

'Some of them, yes,' the Queen replied. 'They are clearly using Diana's death to make as much money as they can.'

Oh dear, thought Blair, this is going to be difficult. 'Normally, I would agree, Ma'am,' he said. 'But I think this is different. People really are unhappy.'

'So what is your advice?'

'Fly the flag at half-mast over Buckingham Palace and come down to London at once, Ma'am. It will help people with their sadness.'

'*Their* sadness? What about my grandchildren's sadness? They have just lost their mother, Mr Blair. I believe that the British people are intelligent enough to realise that sadness is best faced in private, with dignity. The rest of the world expects this kind of dignity from our country.'

Blair felt that he was facing a stone wall. He knew he couldn't change the Queen's opinion. 'If that is your opinion, Ma'am, the government will accept it.' He said goodbye and put the phone down.

It started ringing again almost immediately. This time it was Robin Janvrin. He had been listening to Blair's conversation with the Queen on another phone.

'I'm sorry, Prime Minister,' Janvrin began. 'Her Majesty's position must be very difficult to accept. But you must understand how surprised she is by the public criticisms. It isn't easy being the Head of State. Times were very different when she became Queen. In the world of today, she doesn't really know what to do.'

Blair was glad Janvrin had called. He felt sorry for the Queen. 'I can't promise anything,' he said. 'It's Her Majesty the people want to see, not me. But I'll do what I can to help with the Press.'

'Thank you, Prime Minister. I'm very grateful.'

Blair put the phone down and called his secretary. 'Tell Alistair I want to see him – now. And everything else can wait.'

CHAPTER 7
The stag

Blair's telephone call had upset the Queen. So had the newspaper headlines. Were her people really so unhappy with the Royal Family? The Queen felt she needed to be alone.

She drove into the countryside. It felt good to be in a quiet, beautiful area away from people. The country roads were rough but she was a very good driver. In a few minutes, she reached the river.

It wasn't deep, but the water ran very quickly over rocks and stones. There was a path through the rocks. If she was careful she could drive across to the other side. Confidently, she drove into the water. Seconds later, there was a loud bang, followed by the sound of tearing metal. There was one rock she hadn't seen. Her car had stopped in the middle of the river. She took out her phone and called the head groundsman's office. He answered at once.

'Hello, Thomas,' she said. 'I'm afraid I've done something rather stupid. I tried to cross the river and hit a rock. Now the car won't move.'

'Don't worry, Ma'am. We'll come and get you right now.'

'Thank you. You're so kind.'

The Queen got out of the car, crossed the river carefully, and sat on a rock on the far side.

For the first time in ages, she was away from other people. All she could hear were the sounds of the natural world: birds singing, running water, leaves blowing in the wind. She closed her eyes and listened – and thought about everything that had happened.

Lately, everything had become too much. There had been one piece of bad news after another. Disagreements in the family, shouting. There had been no time to think. In fact, this was the first time she'd really …

Suddenly, the Queen started crying. Away from the world, she could allow her feelings to show.

After a few seconds, she heard a noise in the trees to her right. She sat up straight. No one must see her crying. She dried her eyes and turned to look.

She moved backwards in wonder and surprise. Standing before her was the stag Philip had been looking for. It was huge. It was also extremely beautiful. Its deep brown eyes looked into hers. She felt as if something joined them together. It was a mix of beauty, sadness – and danger. These wonderful animals had lived in the forest for thousands of years. They were something to look at and enjoy. But this was also the animal her husband wanted to kill. Wasn't its position similar to hers? She, too, belonged to something very old: a tradition that went back more than a thousand years. Now that tradition was also in danger. 'Can you and I survive in this modern world?' she wondered. Time seemed to stand still. She couldn't take her eyes away from the animal. She just looked and lost herself in its awesome beauty. It was more like a dream than anything real.

Was it seconds? Or minutes? She didn't know. But the dream was broken by the sound of cars coming closer. Thomas and his men were arriving.

The Queen stood up. She didn't want her men to see the stag. 'Go away!' she shouted, clapping her hands. 'Go on. Go!'

At first, the stag didn't move. It just looked at the Queen. But then, as the noise of the cars got louder, he dropped his head, gave the Queen one last look, and disappeared into the trees.

'Thank God,' she whispered.

Seconds later, Thomas and his men appeared. She waved but she was still thinking of the stag.

They were moments she would never forget.

CHAPTER 8
The decision

The media were crowded outside Blair's house. They told Cherie Blair that the Prime Minister had arranged to speak to them.

She called her husband. 'The news people are outside,' she said as Blair came into the room. 'They told me that you were going to speak to them. What's all that about?'

'I told Robin Janvrin that I would try and help the Queen. The best way I can do that is by speaking to the Press. I want to explain the Queen's position. I'm hoping it will help people understand.'

'I don't understand why you're trying so hard to help her,' she said.

'Because we can't allow the Queen to destroy herself this way. Also, I don't like the ugly way everyone is attacking her.'

Cherie disagreed, but she didn't say anything.

Blair did his best to make the Press understand the Queen's reasons for not coming to London.

Later that day, the Queen watched him answering their questions on TV from her bedroom in Balmoral. When Philip came into the room, her attention turned to the boys.

'How are William and Harry today?' she asked.

'Angry, I'm afraid,' answered Philip. 'They saw the newspapers earlier today.'

The Queen closed her eyes. 'Oh, no,' she said. 'We must be more careful.'

The picture on the TV screen changed. Visitors coming

to Diana's funeral in London were shown sleeping in the streets. Many were crying and lighting candles.

People lighting candles in the streets the night before Princess Diana's funeral

Philip couldn't believe what he was seeing. 'Sleeping in the streets and crying for someone they never even knew? And they think *we* are mad?'

The Queen closed her eyes. Philip's shouting gave her a headache. And it didn't change anything. 'It's very important,' Philip continued, as he got into bed, 'that you don't let Blair tell you what to do. People will soon realise how stupid this whole thing is.'

The Queen didn't reply. She looked at the pictures of modern Britain on the TV screen in front of her. It was a world she didn't understand.

The next morning it was clear that Blair's statements

trying to protect the Queen hadn't worked. Only one newspaper had listened to him and was on the Royal Family's side. The headlines in the others were even worse than the day before.

Campbell read them out to Blair. 'Where is our Queen?'; 'Show us you care!'.

'But there's good news for you!' Campbell picked up another newspaper and read aloud, 'Blair is now more popular than Winston Churchill*.'

'Right,' said Blair. 'I need to speak to the Queen again.' He waved Campbell away, picked up the phone, and called Balmoral.

'Good morning, Ma'am,' he said when the Queen came to the phone. 'If you've seen today's papers, I'm sure you'll agree that things are becoming very serious. They are now saying that one in four people would prefer a Britain without a royal family.' Blair's voice sounded strong and confident. The Queen stayed silent and looked very sad. 'I suggest the following … '

After the telephone conversation, the Queen didn't know what to do. She needed to talk to someone. She went for a walk with her mother in the garden.

'So what does Mr Blair want you to do?' the Queen Mother asked.

'First: fly the flag over Buckingham Palace. Second: fly down to London as soon as possible. Third: visit Diana's coffin. Fourth: give a speech to my people and the world on television. If I do all these things we might – just might – avoid further problems.'

* Winston Churchill was Britain's Prime Minister during the Second World War.

'What does Lord Airlie say?'

'He agrees with Mr Blair.'

'Really?'

'Something's happened. There's been a change. It seems that many of the things I have always believed in aren't important now. I don't understand my people any more. Perhaps it's time to stop being Queen and let someone 'modern' rule instead.'

The Queen Mother stopped. 'Certainly not,' she said. 'You must never say such things. Remember the promise you made to your people: "I will give my whole life to working for you".'

'But if my actions are hurting the Royal Family ... '

'Hurting?' the Queen Mother said in surprise. Her face turned serious. 'You, my dear, are one of the greatest leaders this country has ever had. The real problems will come when you leave, but you don't have to think about that now.'

'But there's a problem *now*. No one seems to think tradition or dignity are important any more. It's all about showing your feelings in public.'

'Yes, but you've never been like that and it's important that you don't change. You are the leader of a tradition more than a thousand years old. Can you imagine any other king or queen going down to London to "help people with their sadness"?'

The Queen didn't answer. She knew she had an important decision to make. She knew what other people thought. Now it was time to be alone.

Her decision came later that afternoon. Robin Janvrin was the first to hear. He telephoned Prince Philip. Philip was out looking for the stag with the boys and the groundsmen. They had been unsuccessful, and were just finishing for the day.

One of the groundsmen took the call. 'Yes, he's here.' He handed the phone to Philip. 'Mr Janvrin for you, Sir.'

Philip was surprised. 'Robin? What is it?' Seconds later, Philip's face turned red. 'What?' he shouted. 'That's madness! The whole thing is complete madness!' He threw down the phone and turned to the rest of the group. 'It seems we are going back to London.'

Charles received the news quite differently. He found his mother in her study. She was working on her speech for TV. 'I believe,' Charles began, 'that you've, er, decided to follow the Prime Minister's advice and go back to London.' The Queen turned away and wouldn't look at him. 'I just wanted to say that I think it's ... er ... a very sensible decision. I just hope we haven't left things too late.'

CHAPTER 9
Returning to London

It didn't take long for the media to hear of the Queen's decision. In less than an hour the gates of Balmoral were crowded with Press and television people. Outside the gates people had laid flowers and cards. The Queen, Charles, Philip and the two young Princes went outside to look at the flowers and read the cards. The Queen seemed uncomfortable with all the cameras around her. Suddenly, there was a loud bang from a passing motorbike. Charles looked up, frightened. He was still afraid of being shot.

Tony Blair was working on papers and watching TV in his living room. He saw the pictures of the Royal Family getting ready to leave Balmoral. 'Thank God for that,' he said.

The Queen was now almost ready to leave Balmoral. She was checking herself in the mirror. Philip stood nearby, shaking his head. 'This isn't right,' he said.

'Perhaps,' the Queen replied, 'but discussing it any more won't help.'

'Oh, well,' said Philip, 'I suppose it'll give the groundsmen time to find another stag.'

The Queen turned pale and stopped. 'Another stag? What do you mean?'

'Oh, didn't you know? The last one walked on to our neighbour's land. One of their guests shot it.'

The Queen felt a cold pain run through her body. She asked the name of the neighbour and where his house was. Philip watched in surprise as she put on an old coat, jumped into her car, and drove off.

Back in London, Alistair Campbell was again reading the day's headlines. 'Downing Street saves the Queen'; 'A quiet word from Tony Blair and the country gets its wish'. Then Campbell began to joke about Blair. He called him 'the father of the country'.

Blair could see that Campbell was enjoying the Queen's weak position. Again, this made him angry but, for the moment, he kept quiet.

The Queen's neighbour was very surprised to see her. He was even more surprised when she asked to see the dead stag.

He showed her the dead animal.

The Queen felt close to the stag. They had both lost something. The stag had lost its life and she had lost the love of her people. She walked over to the animal and touched it softly. 'It was hurt,' she said.

'Yes, one of our guests shot it. He couldn't shoot very well, I'm afraid. He didn't kill the stag. We had to look for it and finish the job ourselves.'

'I hope it wasn't in too much pain,' the Queen said. She turned to her neighbour. 'Thank you for letting me see it.'

'Not at all, Ma'am.'

The Queen left the building with dignity. But like the stag before her, she was hurting, too.

The flight to London in the royal plane was very short. The Queen sat quietly, looking out of the window. On a table in front of her were the day's newspapers with their unkind headlines. To the Queen, it seemed there would be no end to the pain she was feeling.

Janvrin appeared at her side. The Queen looked up.

'I've made a copy of your television speech, Ma'am.' He handed her a paper.

The Queen put on her glasses and began to read. Janvrin felt sorry for her. He wanted to say something to make her feel better. But the words wouldn't come. 'Was there anything else?' the Queen asked.

'No, Ma'am. Just that we'll be landing in fifteen minutes.'

'Thank you,' she said.

CHAPTER 10
The Queen talks to her people

Alistair Campbell watched the TV pictures of the Royal Family driving from the airport to Buckingham Palace. A secretary walked in the room carrying a copy of the Queen's television speech.

Campbell looked up. 'It's a copy of the Queen's speech,' said the secretary. 'For Tony.'

'Let me have a look at it first,' Campbell said. He pulled the papers from her hand.

As the Royal Family drove nearer to the Palace, they realised, for the first time, the size of the crowds. They were huge. But were they also unfriendly? The Queen was worried. She didn't understand her people any more and felt afraid and alone.

The crowds were silent as the Queen and Prince Philip stopped in front of Buckingham Palace and stepped out of the car. They looked at the flowers and read some of the cards lining the wall. One of the cards read: 'You were too good for them'. 'Them' was clearly the Royal Family. The Queen was hurt by these words but, as always, tried to hide her feelings.

She turned to the crowd. A little girl held out some flowers.

'Would you like me to put them with the others for you?' the Queen asked.

'No,' said the little girl. But before the Queen could feel hurt by that, the little girl added, 'These flowers are for you,' and gave them to the Queen. The Queen was so grateful she felt like crying.

Blair and his assistants watched the Queen on TV. Campbell came into the room and gave some papers to Blair. 'It's the Queen's speech,' he said. 'I made a few changes. I had to, if we want to make her sound like a real person.' Blair began to look angry. He hated the way Campbell took every chance to attack the Queen. 'Oh, and you'll be happy to know,' Campbell continued, 'that the old woman's finally agreed to visit Diana's coffin.'

For Blair, this was too much. He stood up, angrily. 'You know what, Alistair?' he said. 'When you get things wrong, you really get them wrong. That "old woman" has given her life to work for the people of this country. She's worked for us for the last forty-four years with unselfishness and dignity. And now everyone's attacking her. For what? For Diana, a young woman who spent most of her time trying to destroy her?' Still angry, Blair turned and left the room.

The visit to Buckingham Palace was over. The Queen was now in the television centre preparing for her speech. She sat in a corner of the room, reading through it.

Janvrin walked over with another piece of paper in his hand. 'Your Majesty,' he began, nervously. 'Er, there's been a last minute addition to your speech, from Downing Street.' He handed her the paper. 'They are suggesting adding "as a grandmother" just here.' Janvrin pointed to a sentence on the paper.

'Right,' said the Queen. She made a note on her copy of the address and then began to read. 'So what I say to you now, as your Queen and as a grandmother ... '

'Do you think you can say that?' Janvrin asked.

'Do I have a choice?' she replied.

One of the television men called her over. An assistant checked her hair and make up. Everything was now ready. The Queen held the speech in front of her as the seconds disappeared. Five, four, three, two, one.

'Since last Sunday's terrible news,' the Queen began, 'people in Britain and all over the world have shown their sadness at Diana's death.'

While millions of people all over the world watched the Queen on their TV's, Philip and Charles watched from the side of the television cameras. Charles looked nervous. Philip looked angry.

In Downing Street, Tony and Cherie Blair watched from their private apartment.

'We have all had to face the feelings that this brings,' the Queen continued. 'Sadness, disbelief, worry about those she left behind. And we have all had to manage these feelings in our own ways. So what I say to you now, as your Queen – and as a grandmother – I say from my heart … '

'Heart? She hasn't got a heart,' said Cherie Blair. 'She doesn't mean any of this.'

'That's not important,' Blair replied. 'She is simply doing the right thing. And that,' he went on, pointing at the television, 'is how you survive.'

Cherie turned to her husband. 'Listen to you,' she said. 'A week ago you were talking about changing things. You were the country's great "modern man". Now you've become romantic over the Queen!'

Blair watched as the Queen reached the end of her speech. 'I hope that tomorrow, we can all join together in showing our sadness at Diana's death. We also thank God for someone who made many, many people very happy.'

CHAPTER 11
A beautiful sister

Almost three million people came to London on the day of Diana's funeral in Westminster Abbey. Many of the world's famous people were there, too. The newspapers were full of pictures of actors, popular musicians and other celebrities. They all looked sad and serious.

The streets near the Abbey were filled with huge television screens. Cameras inside the church would carry pictures of the service to the people waiting outside.

The night before the funeral, there was a strange calm over London. Many people slept in the city's streets and parks.

Morning came. The day was clear and sunny. At ten o'clock, Diana's coffin started its journey to Westminster Abbey. Many people cried, covered their faces with their hands or put an arm around a friend. Even strangers came together in sadness.

In the middle of all this, the Queen and the Royal Family looked uncomfortable. They sat with important guests and members of Diana's family in Westminster Abbey. Diana's brother, Earl Spencer, was about to begin his speech for Diana. Radio and television carried his words to the crowds outside.

'My sister, Diana, was a very British girl,' Spencer began. 'But at the same time, she was international and without class. She would help anyone, rich or poor. And she didn't need a royal title to do good things. Diana died as a very beautiful woman with happiness in her private life. I would like to thank God for that. But, most of all, I want to give thanks for the life of a woman I am very proud to call my sister. Her beauty will never leave us.'

Earl Spencer's speech on TV screens outside Westminster Abbey

At the end of the speech, people outside the church started clapping. The clapping got louder. People inside the church started clapping, too. Tony Blair began clapping too. The Queen looked down. She felt more uncomfortable than ever. It was simply not right to clap in church. Would this day never end?

CHAPTER 12
Looking back

The summer was over. Diana's funeral was two months ago but it seemed longer. Britain's new government was just starting the serious business of managing the country. Its leader, Tony Blair, was getting ready for his weekly meeting in Buckingham Palace with the Queen. He checked his appearance in the mirror.

'So,' said Cherie, walking into the room. 'Are you going to see your girlfriend?'

'Now, now, don't joke,' Blair replied.

Cherie smiled and straightened his tie. 'Well, I just hope she's grateful. She should be. You saved the Royal Family.'

'I don't think she sees things that way,' said Blair.

When Blair arrived at the Palace, Robin Janvrin was there to welcome him.

'Good morning, Prime Minister,' said Janvrin, shaking Blair's hand.

Blair smiled. 'Please, call me Tony.'

Janvrin smiled to himself. He remembered the Queen's dislike of Blair's idea of using first names. But Blair hadn't noticed. He was following one of the Queen's servants up the stairs. The man knocked at the door of the Queen's room, then opened it and stepped aside as Blair entered. Blair smiled at the Queen. He looked happy and confident.

These feelings didn't last. When he went to shake the Queen's hand she took it away rather quickly.

Blair sat down and said, 'It's nice to see you again. After a rather interesting summer.' The Queen looked at him. 'I'm talking about your trip to India and Pakistan,' Blair continued quickly. 'The things you said about ending old disagreements were very successful.' Blair looked at the Queen and smiled.

The Queen didn't reply. She disliked the way Blair was saying nice things about her. She knew he only wanted her to like him.

Blair was feeling more and more uncomfortable. 'It's the first time I've seen you since … that week,' he said.

The Queen looked up suddenly. 'And I wanted to say sorry,' Blair continued.

'What for?' asked the Queen, looking surprised.

'I didn't want you to feel that you had been ... er, *managed* in any way.'

'Certainly not. But I don't think I will ever understand what happened in the summer.'

'Well, it was a very unusual time,' said Blair. 'And I think history will show it was a very good week for you, Ma'am.'

'And an even better week for you, Mr Blair,' she said.

'But there are 52 weeks in a year, Your Majesty. People will forget those few days.'

'Oh, really?' said the Queen. 'You don't think that people have a lower opinion now of the Royal Family than they had before the summer?'

'Not at all, Ma'am.'

Blair's false smiles didn't make the Queen feel any better. 'I understand,' she said, quietly, 'that some of your closest advisors were quite happy to attack us.'

Again Blair looked uncomfortable. 'One or two, maybe. But, as leader, I could never agree with them.'

'You are very kind, Mr Blair. But we mustn't forget your private reasons.'

'Private reasons, Ma'am?'

'You felt that one day, the same thing could happen to you.' Blair tried to speak but couldn't. He looked uneasy as the Queen continued. 'And it will, Mr Blair. Quite suddenly, when you least expect it.' She stood up. 'But enough of that. Let's get on with our business.' She walked over to the window. 'Oh, look,' she said. 'I do love this time of day. Shall we take a walk in the garden while it's still light? I do hope you are a walker, Mr Blair.'

'Er, yes,' Blair replied. He still looked uneasy.

On their way downstairs the Queen suddenly stopped and turned to Blair. 'Did you say one in four people wanted me to go?'

'Only for about half an hour,' said Blair. 'But then you came down to London and everything was OK again.'

'One in four,' the Queen said slowly. 'You know, I've never been hated like that.' She looked very sad.

'I imagine that was difficult.'

'Yes,' the Queen replied, quietly. 'Very. I thought people wanted a Queen who felt that her duty to her people was more important than private feelings. I was wrong. I can see that the world has changed. And I suppose we must become more "modern".'

'Well, perhaps I can help,' said Blair. He was looking more confident again.

'Don't get too confident, Mr Blair. Remember, *I* am the one who is supposed to be advising *you*.' She gave him a kind look, and they both laughed.

The Queen called her dogs. They led her and Blair into the Palace garden.

'So,' said the Queen when they were outside. 'What can I expect from your government?'

'Well, top of our list is education. We want to make class sizes smaller ...'

Robin Janvrin watched Blair and the Queen from one of the windows. Blair was explaining his plans like an excited schoolboy. Her Majesty listened as she walked. Janvrin smiled to himself. The problems of the summer were behind her. Once again, she looked calm, strong, and confident. And this was how he would always remember her. Royal and proud – the perfect Queen.

The Success of *The Queen*

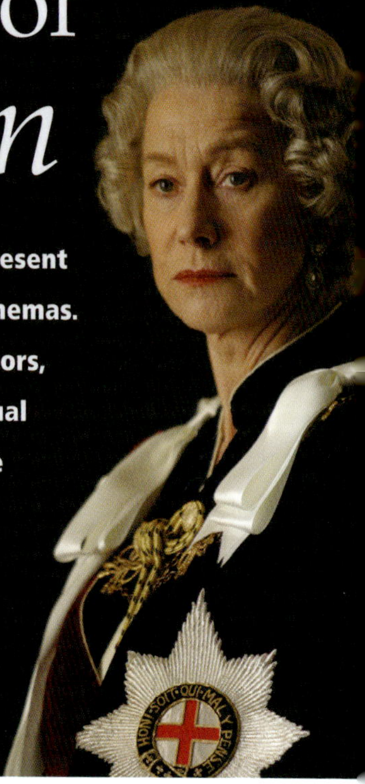

***The Queen* was the first film about the present British royal family to appear in world cinemas. Thanks to the writer, director, and the actors, it was a huge success. But it was an unusual subject. So why did anyone want to make a film about the royal family?**

Writer Peter Morgan wanted his story to be as close to the truth as possible. To do this, he spoke to people who worked for both the Queen and Tony Blair's government. He also spoke to people who had stayed at Balmoral as guests. The result is a story that gives a clear picture of the Queen and the royal family during a difficult time.

Stephen Frears, the director, didn't want people to think his film was unfair to the Queen. His film describes the problems between modern and traditional ways of managing the death of Princess Diana. But through it all, Frears shows the Queen as a person who has great feeling and dignity.

Helen Mirren

Helen Mirren is known throughout the world as a very fine actress.

After watching Helen Mirren as the Queen, the audience at the *Venice Film Festival* stood and clapped for five minutes. Helen had earned her success. 'I studied old news films of the Queen very carefully,' she said. 'I wanted to get everything right – the voice, the hair, the hands - everything.'

Helen loved playing the part of the Queen. But she also said she had never been so nervous of a part before.

The Queen won the BAFTA (*The British Academy of Film and Television Arts*) award in 2007 for the year's best film. It was also nominated for an *Academy Award*. But the most awards went to Helen Mirren and Peter Morgan. Helen won 29 awards, including an Oscar for *Best Actress*. Peter won 11 awards, including the *Golden Globe* for best screenplay.

Imagine you have to choose an actor for the 'Best Actor' award. Who would you give it to, and why?

Helen Mirren

Before *The Queen* was filmed, Helen also invited the other main actors to spend time together as a family at her house. This made acting together easier and more natural.

Michael Sheen

Michael Sheen played Tony Blair in *The Queen*. He had already played this part in an earlier film called *The Deal*.

Michael Sheen

James Cromwell

More than two metres tall, the American actor James Cromwell was the perfect person to play the part of the Queen's tall husband, Prince Philip.

James Cromwell

What do these words mean? You can use a dictionary.

audience director award screenplay nominate producer festival

The British Monarchy

For more than a thousand years, England's kings and queens have been the heads of state of Great Britain and the countries of the Commonwealth. But what is the role of the Queen and the royal family in the 21st century?

For many British people, the Queen is an example of what is good and unchanging about the United Kingdom. As head of the oldest monarchy in the world, she tries to show her people that tradition, dignity, and doing your duty, is still important in modern life.

The Queen is the most-travelled monarch in history. She and Prince Philip often make state visits to other countries. These visits help to keep friendly feelings between the United Kingdom and the rest of the world.

Elizabeth Alexandra Mary Windsor

Born: April 21, 1926.

Became Queen: June 2, 1953.

Head of state: of sixteen countries, including Australia, Canada and New Zealand.

Interests: horse racing, photography and her dogs

Political views: She's never given a public opinion.

Does your country have a royal family? Can royal families still be useful in modern times?

The Queen's days are very busy. Her duties include answering letters, reading state papers and meeting important people. She also visits places which do valuable work such as hospitals, schools, universities, and museums.

University, Scotland, in 2006, where he studied History of Art. Like his brother, Prince Harry is very interested in sports. He plays rugby and polo. He has a career in the army, and received a medal for the time he spent as a soldier in Afghanistan.

Others in the royal family also have public visits and duties. These public events show that the royal family care about what happens in the world and can still play a helpful part today.

What is the future of the royal family? No one is certain. Traditionally, Prince Charles is the next in line to be King, and after him, Prince William.

Prince William finished his university studies at St Andrews

What do these words mean? You can use a dictionary.

monarchy role Commonwealth polo career army medal

Princess Diana

By the time of her tragic death, on August 31, 1997, Princess Diana had become the most celebrated woman on Earth. She was also described as 'the world's most photographed woman'. Her picture was always on the covers of magazines like *Time*, *People*, and *Newsweek*. What was so special about Princess Diana? Why was she so popular?

Diana's early years

Diana was born on July 1, 1961. She was the third child of Edward and Frances Spencer, an aristocratic English family. When Diana was eight, her parents divorced and she went to live with her father. In 1976, her father married again. These were difficult years for Diana and she spent a lot of time travelling between her two parents' homes.

During her school years, Diana was a good swimmer and dancer. But she was a poor student. She left school in 1977, after failing all her exams. When she began going out with Prince Charles, she was working as an assistant in a nursery school in London.

An unhappy marriage

Diana married Prince Charles on July 29, 1981. Over a billion people watched the wedding on TV all over the world. The media described Charles and Diana as 'the perfect couple'.

This wasn't true. In time, their different personalities produced problems in the marriage. Charles was still in love with his old girlfriend, Camilla Parker-Bowles, and he and Diana spent less time together. These problems between Charles and Diana were interesting

to everyone, and newspapers made a lot of money from stories about the royal couple. The media spoke to Charles and Diana's friends and, finally, to the couple themselves.

The Queen wasn't happy about all this media attention on the royal family. She asked the couple to divorce. They agreed and were divorced on August 28, 1996.

The People's Princess

Diana was not a perfect royal. She made mistakes. She showed her feelings too much in public. Through the media, she became a celebrity. She became famous for her charity work. None of this was the 'royal' way of doing things. But this only made her more popular with the public.

Like many ordinary people in the world, Diana had a difficult background, an unhappy marriage, and a wish to help others. The public saw her as a beautiful, caring, open woman. Ordinary people loved her, and they accepted her faults as much as they celebrated her beauty. Why was this? 'Because,' as one woman said, 'Diana is like us.' This, more than anything, made her 'the People's Princess'.

What do these words mean? You can use a dictionary.
tragic **aristocratic** **nursery school** **couple**

INTRODUCTION & CHAPTERS 1–4

Before you read

You can use a dictionary for this section.

1 Look at the New Words in the back of the book.

a) Which of these words describe someone who is popular and famous? **a celebrity** **a servant** **an ambassador**

b) Which of these is about helping others less lucky than yourself? **dignity** **duty** **charity**

c) Which of these describes only the newspaper and magazine world? **media** **press** **public**

d) Which of these is about the correct way to act with important people? **royal** **tradition** **protocol**

e) Which one of these do you have when you choose a new government? **a funeral** **a speech** **an election**

f) Which of these is an animal? **a coffin** **a stag** **an institution**

2 Complete the sentences with these words.

Ambassador **coffin** **divorced** **institution** **public** **royal** **speech** **tradition**

a) They're not married any more. They got .... last year.

b) She wanted to say something good about her father's life so she wrote a ....

c) Anyone can come to the show. It's open to the ....

d) They put the dead body in a wooden ....

e) The Prince and Princess got married last Saturday. Thirty million people watched the .... wedding.

f) He works for the British government in another country. He is the British Foreign ....

g) The church is Italy's oldest religious ....

h) The .... here is to always eat fish on Fridays.

After you read

You can use a dictionary for this section.

3 Answer the questions.

a) Why was Diana unhappy in the mid-1980s?

b) Does Cherie Blair think Britain should have a royal family?

c) In Chapter 2, why is Charles angry with his mother?

d) Why does the Queen ask her servants to take the radio and TV out of her grandchildren's rooms?

e) Earl Spencer spoke about his sister's death. Whose fault did he think her death was?

f) What does the Queen think of Blair's idea to have a public funeral for Diana?

g) Why does the Queen ask Philip not to take guns to Craggy Head?

h) Whose idea was the title, 'the People's Princess'?

i) Why do Prince Charles and Tony Blair shake hands for a second time at the airport?

4 What do you think?

a) Will the Queen change her views about having a private funeral for Diana? Why, or why not?

CHAPTERS 5–8

Before you read

You can use a dictionary for this section.

5 Match the words with the definitions.

a) a flag	**i)** someone whose job is to look after private land
b) a headline	**ii)** a symbol of a country
c) criticism	**iii)** when someone expresses negative views about a situation or someone's actions.
d) a groundsman	**iv)** the title of the main story in a newspaper

6 What's going to happen next? Have a guess!

a) Will the public forgive the Queen now that she has decided to have a public funeral for Diana?

b) Will the Queen show sadness about Diana's death, on TV or in the newspapers?

After you read

7 Are these sentences true or false? Correct the false sentences.

a) Campbell thinks Charles is afraid someone will shoot him.

b) The Queen wants to spend time alone with Charles.

c) Philip never wanted Charles to marry Diana.

d) Blair thinks that Britain should stop having a royal family.

e) Janvrin tries to help the Queen by speaking to Blair.

f) The Queen thinks the Press are using Diana's death to make money.

g) The Queen hates being alone.

8 What do you think?

a) Why does the Queen think she is similar to the stag? Do you agree with her opinion? Why, or why not?

CHAPTERS 9–12

Before you read

You can use a dictionary for this section.

9 The Queen has decided to go to London. How do you think these people will feel about her decision?

a) Tony Blair **b)** Alistair Campbell

c) The Queen Mother **d)** The people of Britain

e) Cherie Blair

10 Use these words to complete the sentences. You may have to change the form of the word.

celebrity clap coffin servant service

a) During the church .... , people sang songs to remember Diana.

b) The speech was so good that everyone .... when it was over.

c) Everyone watched sadly as the .... was put into the ground at the funeral.

d) One of the .... took the visitors upstairs to see the Queen.

e) Singers, actors and other .... came to Diana's funeral.

After you read

11 Who says these things? Who are they speaking to?

a) ' ... discussing it any more won't help.'

b) 'He didn't kill the stag.'

c) 'These flowers are for you.'

d) 'When you get things wrong, you *really* get them wrong.'

e) 'Do you think you can say that?'

f) 'She hasn't got a heart.'

g) 'Are you going to see your girlfriend?'

h) 'I've never been hated like that.'

12 What do you think?

a) What lesson does the Queen want Tony Blair to learn from her experience with the public and the media during the days after Diana's death?